My Classic Stories

Hansel
and
Gretel

This book belongs to

Age - - - - - - - - - -

Enjoy this book,
love from Hansel and Gretel

This edition first published in 2013 by Ginger Fox Ltd
Copyright © 2013 Ginger Fox Ltd

Published in the UK by:
Ginger Fox Ltd
Stirling House, College Road
Cheltenham GL53 7HY
United Kingdom

www.gingerfox.co.uk

Retold by Nina Filipek
Illustrated by Jacqueline East

ISBN: 978-0-9557785-7-5

10 9 8 7 6 5 4 3 2 1

Printed and bound in China.

Hansel
and
Gretel

Once upon a time there was a boy called Hansel and a girl called Gretel.

They lived with their father, who was a poor woodcutter, and their cruel stepmother. Often they went to bed hungry.

One night, they heard
their stepmother say,

"We have only enough food
for ourselves. Tomorrow we will
have to take the children into the
woods and leave them there."

Gretel cried and cried,
but Hansel had a plan.

"Don't worry," he said to Gretel.
"I will look after you."

Once everyone was asleep, Hansel
crept outside and filled his pockets
with white pebbles. Then he went
back to bed.

The next day,
their stepmother and father
took them into the woods.
Hansel stayed back, and as they
walked along, he dropped the
pebbles onto the path.

When they were in the
middle of the woods, their
father made a big fire.

Their stepmother told them
that she and their father
were going to collect
more wood. She told the
children they would come
back for them later.

But they did not come back.

Gretel began to cry.

Hansel said, "Don't worry.
When the moon comes out we
will find our way home."

At last the moon came out, and the white pebbles shone brightly in the moonlight. Hansel and Gretel followed the trail of pebbles all the way back home!

When their father saw them he was so pleased.

Their stepmother,
however, was not happy.
That night, they heard her say,

"Tomorrow we will have
to take the children deeper
into the woods and leave
them there."

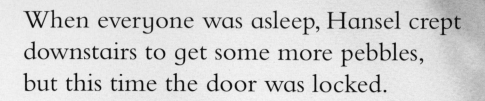

When everyone was asleep, Hansel crept downstairs to get some more pebbles, but this time the door was locked.

He went back to bed empty-handed and very sad.

The next day, their stepmother woke them up early.

She gave them each a piece of bread.
Then she took them deep into the woods.

As they walked along, Hansel
dropped crumbs of bread onto the
path behind them.

They reached the
deepest part of the
woods, where their
stepmother told them to
wait. She said she would
come back for them later.
Hansel and Gretel waited,
but she did not come back.

Gretel shared her bread
with Hansel, and soon
it grew dark.

Hansel said, "Don't worry. When the moon comes out we will follow the trail of breadcrumbs home."

At last, the moon came out. But Hansel and Gretel could not see the breadcrumbs.

The hungry birds had eaten them all!

Hansel and Gretel were lost in
the woods, and spent the night
huddled together. The next day
when they awoke, they saw a white
bird singing in a tree. It had such a
lovely call that they followed it.
The white bird led them to the
strangest cottage.

They could not believe their eyes!
The cottage was made of gingerbread and
sweets of every kind.

The children were so hungry that they
broke off sweets to eat, and failed to
notice the old woman watching them.

The cottage door opened
and the old woman came out.

She invited them inside and gave them pancakes,
but she was only pretending to be nice.

Really she was a wicked witch!

The **wicked witch** locked Hansel in a cage, and she made Gretel scrub the floor.

Every day the **wicked witch** fed Hansel huge meals. She was fattening him up to eat him!

21

So Hansel played a trick on her!

When she reached in the cage to feel how fat he was, he stuck out a chicken bone.

The wicked witch had bad eyesight – so she thought it was his finger. She was disappointed that he was not getting any fatter.

One day, the wicked witch decided to eat
Hansel anyway – even if he was too thin.
She told Gretel to get into the oven to
check that it was hot enough. She was
really planning to eat Gretel as well!

Clever Gretel pretended she did not know how.
So the wicked witch said she would show her.
Gretel saw her chance. She shoved the
wicked witch inside the oven and
quickly locked the door.

Then she freed Hansel from the cage.

Hansel and Gretel found some precious pearls in the wicked witch's house.

"These are better than pebbles!" said Hansel. "We can take them back for father." So he put some pearls in his pocket.

They left the cottage and at last they found the path home.

Their father was overjoyed to see them again, and told them that their stepmother had died while they were gone.

Hansel gave him the pearls from the wicked witch's house. They were able to buy lots of food with the pearls, and they all lived happily ever after.

Can you remember?

Now that you have read the story, try
to answer these questions about it.

1. Why did their stepmother want to leave
   Hansel and Gretel in the woods?

2. What did Hansel do with the pebbles he collected?

3. Why couldn't the children follow
   the breadcrumbs to get back home?

4. How did Hansel trick the **wicked witch**?

5. What was the **wicked witch**'s
   cottage made from? Was it:

   gingerbread
   and
   sweets?

   OR

   sausage
   and
   mash?

Did you spot?

Hansel and Gretel did not see the
wicked witch watching them, but how
much did you notice?

1. Did you spot the **wicked witch's** cat chasing the mouse?

2. How many rabbits can you count?

3. Did you notice the two wide-eyed owls up in the branches?

4. Can you spot the **wicked witch** hiding in her gingerbread house?

5. What was the name of the **wicked witch's** cookbook?

6. "How many birds as well as me are in the woods?"

Complete your collection ...

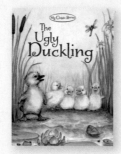 The Ugly Duckling

 The Three Billy Goats Gruff

 Hansel and Gretel

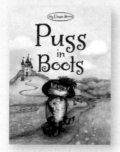 Puss in Boots

 Little Red Riding Hood

 Jack and the Beanstalk

 Cinderella

 The Gingerbread Man

 The Emperor's New Clothes

 Goldilocks and the Three Bears

 Rapunzel

 The Three Little Pigs

"Which one will you read next?"